小矮人與鞋匠
The Elves and the Shoemaker

retold by Henriette Barkow
illustrated by Jago

Chinese translation by Sylvia Denham

Withdrawn for sale

從前有一個鞋匠和他的妻子，他很勤勞工作，但是因為時尚的改變，
人們不再買他的皮鞋，他越來越貧窮，最後他只剩下足夠造一
雙皮鞋的皮革。

Once there lived a shoemaker and his wife. He worked hard, but fashions
changed and people didn't buy his shoes any more. He became poorer and
poorer. In the end he only had enough leather to make one last pair of shoes.

剪剪，切切！他切割出
兩隻皮鞋的模樣。

Snip, snip! He cut out the shape
of two shoes.

他把它們放在工作檯上，
準備第二天早上開始縫製。

He left them on the workbench ready
to start sewing in the morning.

第二日，當鞋匠走下樓時，他看到⋯
一雙美麗的皮鞋，
他把它們拿起，看到每一針都是恰當的縫造。
「不知道這雙皮鞋是誰造的呢？」他想道。

The next day, when he came downstairs, he found… a beautiful pair of shoes.
He picked them up and saw that every stitch was perfectly sewn.
"I wonder who made these shoes?" he thought.

就在這時，一位女士走進鞋店。「那雙皮鞋真漂亮，」
她說，「那需要多少錢？」
鞋匠告訴她價錢，但是她卻給鞋匠雙倍的價錢。

Just then a woman came in to the shop. "Those shoes are gorgeous,"
she said. "How much are they?"
The shoemaker told her the price but she gave him twice the money
he had asked for.

現在鞋匠有足夠的金錢去買
食物和一些皮革，他準備造
兩雙皮鞋。

Now the shoemaker had
enough money to buy food
and some leather to make
two pairs of shoes.

剪剪，切切！剪剪，切切！
他切割出四隻皮鞋的模樣。

Snip, snip! Snip, snip!
He cut out the shapes of four shoes.

他把它們放在工作檯上，
準備第二天早上開始縫製。

He left them on the workbench ready
to start sewing in the morning.

第二日，當鞋匠走下樓時，他看到… 兩雙美麗的皮鞋，
「不知道這些皮鞋是誰造的呢？」他想道。
就在這時，一對男女走進鞋店，「看看那些鞋子，」那男人說。
「一雙給你，一雙給我，它們需要多少錢？」那女人問道。
鞋匠告訴他們價錢，但是他們卻給鞋匠雙倍的價錢。

The next day, when he came down the stairs, he found... two beautiful pairs of shoes.
"I wonder who made these shoes?" he thought.
Just then a couple came in to the shop. "Look at those shoes," said the man.
"There is one pair for you and one pair for me. How much are they?" asked the woman.
The shoemaker told them the price, but they gave him twice the money he had asked for.

現在鞋匠有足夠的金錢去買更多的食物和一些皮革，他準被造四雙皮鞋。

Now the shoemaker had enough money to buy more food and some leather to make four pairs of shoes.

剪剪，切切！剪剪，切切！剪剪，切切！
剪剪，切切！他切割出八隻皮鞋的模樣。
他把它們放在工作檯上，準備第二天早上
開始縫製。

Snip, snip! Snip, snip! Snip, snip! Snip, snip!
He cut out the shapes of eight shoes. He left them on
the workbench ready to start sewing in the morning.

第二日，當鞋匠走下樓時，他看到⋯ 四雙美麗的皮鞋，
「不知道這些皮鞋是誰造的呢？」他想道。
就在這時，一家男女老少走進鞋店，「啊！看看那些鞋子，」男孩說。
「一雙給你，一雙給我，」女孩說道。
「一雙給媽媽，一雙給爸爸，」男孩說。
「它們需要多少錢？」孩子的父母問道。鞋匠告訴他們價錢，但是他們卻給鞋匠雙倍的價錢。

The next day when he came down the stairs he found... four beautiful pairs of shoes.
"I wonder who made these shoes?" he thought.
Just then a family came in to the shop.
"Wow! Look at those shoes!" said the boy.
"There is a pair for you and a pair for me," said the girl.
"And a pair for mum and a pair for dad," said the boy.
"How much are they?" asked the parents. The shoemaker told them the price, but they gave him twice the money he had asked for.

現在每一天晚上，鞋匠都會為新鞋切割皮革，而第二天的早上，各種不同式樣和尺碼的漂亮皮鞋便會恰當的縫製好 – 有適合男士的皮鞋，也有適合女士的皮鞋，有男孩子的皮鞋，也有女孩子的皮鞋，大的皮鞋，小的皮鞋，皮靴和拖鞋，它們是世界上最完美的鞋子。

Now every evening the shoemaker would cut out the leather for new shoes and every morning there would be perfectly stitched beautiful shoes of all shapes and sizes - shoes for men and shoes for women, shoes for boys and shoes for girls, big shoes and small shoes, boots and slippers. They were the best shoes in the land.

當晚間逐漸延長和逐漸寒冷時，鞋匠坐著細想究竟是誰縫製這些皮鞋。

剪剪，切切！剪剪，切切！鞋匠為皮鞋切割皮革。

「我知道了，」他對妻子說，「我們不去睡覺，看看是誰造我們的皮鞋。」於是鞋匠和他的妻子便躲到架子的後面。

到了午夜時分，兩個小矮人出現。

As the nights became longer and colder the shoemaker sat and thought about who could be making the shoes.
Snip, snip! Snip, snip! The shoemaker cut out the leather for the shoes.
"I know," he said to his wife, "let's stay up and find out who is making our shoes." So the shoemaker and his wife hid behind the shelves.
On the stroke of midnight, two little men appeared.

他們坐在鞋匠的工作檯上，
嗖！嗖！他們開始釘縫。

They sat at the shoemaker's bench.
Swish, swish! They sewed.

啪，啪！他們錘擊著，他們的小指
頭工作快速，鞋匠簡直不能相信他
的眼睛。

Tap, tap! They hammered in the
nails. Their little fingers worked
so fast that the shoemaker
could hardly believe his eyes.

嗖，嗖！啪，啪！他們一直不停的工作，直至最後的一塊皮革造成鞋子為止，
他們跟著便跳下來走了。

Swish, swish! Tap, tap! They didn't stop until every piece of leather had been made into shoes.
Then, they jumped down and ran away.

「哦，那些可憐的小矮人！他們的衣服破舊，一定是
很冷的了，」鞋匠的妻子説道，
「他們的辛勤工作幫了我們很多，但是卻甚麼也沒有，
我們一定要為他們做一些事。」
「你認爲我們應該做甚麼？」鞋匠問道。
「我知道，」他的妻子説，「我為他們造一些溫暖的衣服。」
「我為他們冰冷赤裸的腳造一些鞋子，」鞋匠説。

"Oh, those poor little men! They must be so cold in those rags," said the wife.
"They have helped us with all their hard work and they have nothing.
We must do something for them."
"What do you think we should do?" asked the shoemaker.
"I know," said the wife. "I will make them some warm clothes to wear."
"And I will make them some shoes for their cold, bare feet," said the shoemaker.

第二天早上，鞋匠和他的妻子沒有像平常一般開店，
他們整天工作，但不是賣皮鞋。

The next morning the shoemaker and his wife didn't open the shop as usual.
They spent the whole day working but it wasn't selling shoes.

嘎噠，嗒！鞋匠的妻子
編織了兩件小毛衣。
嘎噠，嗒！她編織了兩對
羊毛襪子。

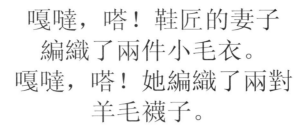

Clickety, click! The shoemaker's
wife knitted two small jumpers.
Clickety, click! She knitted two
pairs of woolly socks.

嗖，嗖！嗖，嗖！
她縫製了兩條溫暖的褲子。

Swish, swish! Swish, swish!
She sewed two pairs of warm trousers.

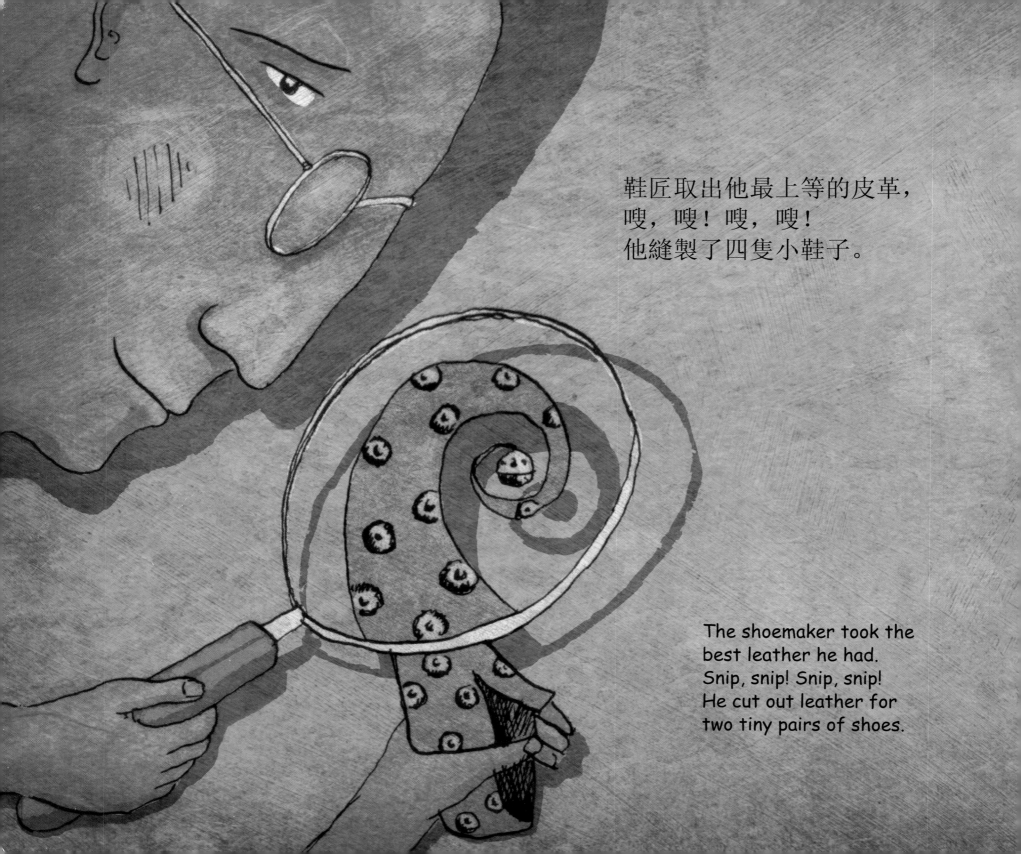

鞋匠取出他最上等的皮革，
嗖，嗖！嗖，嗖！
他縫製了四隻小鞋子。

The shoemaker took the
best leather he had.
Snip, snip! Snip, snip!
He cut out leather for
two tiny pairs of shoes.

嗖，嗖！嗖，嗖！
他縫製了四隻小鞋子。
啪，啪！啪，啪！
他為每雙皮鞋錘擊鞋底。
它們都是他一生以來造得最好的皮鞋。

Swish, swish! Swish, swish!
He stitched four small shoes.
Tap, tap! Tap, tap!
He hammered the soles onto each pair.
They were the best shoes he had ever made.

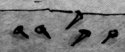

那天晚上，鞋匠的妻子將兩件毛衣、兩條褲子和兩對襪子放在工作檯上。鞋匠把四隻完美的皮鞋取代平時造鞋的皮革，放在工作檯上，跟著他們便躲進架子的後面等候。

That evening the shoemaker's wife placed two jumpers, two pairs of trousers and two pairs of socks on the workbench. The shoemaker placed four perfect shoes on the workbench instead of the leather for making shoes. Then they hid behind the shelves and waited.

到了午夜時分，兩個小矮人出現，並準備工作，
但是當他們看到衣服時，他們停下來凝視，跟著
便迅速地把衣服穿上。

On the stroke of midnight the two little men appeared ready for work.
But when they saw the clothes they stopped and stared.
Then they quickly put them on.

他們高興得拍起手掌 – 啪，啪！
他們高興得跳躂雙腳 – 噠，噠！
他們在店內跳舞，並跳出店外，
他們究竟跳到那裡去，我們永遠也不會知道。

They were so happy they clapped their hands - clap clap!
They were so happy they tapped their feet - tap tap!
They danced around the shop and out of the door.
And where they went we'll never know.

Key Words

elves	小矮人	sewing	縫製
shoemaker	鞋匠	making	製造
wife	妻子	gorgeous	漂亮
shop	店鋪	price	價錢
fashions	時尚	money	金錢
shoe	鞋子	cut out	切割出
shoes	鞋子	stitch	釘縫
poor	貧窮	day	日間
leather	皮革	morning	早上
pair	一雙	evening	晚上
workbench	工作檯	nights	晚間

詞語

midnight	午夜	socks	襪子
stroke	敲擊	clapped	拍手
stay up	不睡覺	tapped	跳躂
hammered	錘擊	danced	跳舞
rags	破舊衣服		
cold	寒冷		
bare	赤裸		
soles	鞋底		
knitted	編織		
jumper	毛衣		
trousers	褲子		

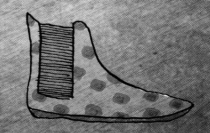

The books on this page have been Pen enabled.
Please touch the Pen to the left hand corner of the page for further information on language availability or visit www.mantralingua.com

TalkingPEN™

علي بابا والاربعين حرامي

Ali Baba
and the *Forty Thieves*

Essebor Attard
Richard Holland

Arabic & English

Ricitos de Oro y los tres ositos

Goldilocks and the Three Bears

Kate Clynes
Louise Daykin

Spanish & English

اللفتة العملاقة
The Giant Turnip

Adapted by Henriette Barkow
Illustrated by Richard Johnson

Arabic & English

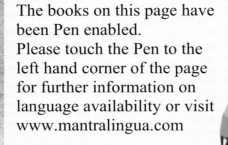

LA PETITE POULE ROUGE ET LES GRAINS DE BLE
The Little Red Hen
and the Grains of Wheat

L. R. Hen
Jago

French & English

LION FABLES
by JAN ORMEROD

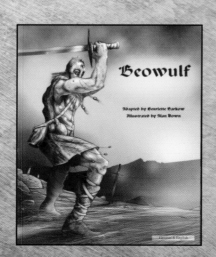

Beowulf

Adapted by Henriette Barkow
Illustrated by Alan Down

German & English

The Children of Lir

Dawn Casey & Diana Mayo

Неужели опять,
Красная Шапочка!

Not Again, Red Riding Hood!

Kate Clynes & Louise Daykin

Russian & English

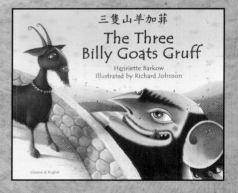

三隻山羊加菲

The Three
Billy Goats Gruff

Henriette Barkow
Illustrated by Richard Johnson

Chinese & English

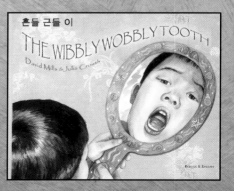

흔들 근들 이
THE WIBBLY WOBBLY TOOTH
David Mills & Julia Crouth

Korean & English